Toot & Puddle

Let it Snow

by Holly Hobbie

LB

LITTLE, BROWN AND COMPANY

New York   Boston

Little, Brown and Company

Hachette Book Group
1290 Avenue of the Americas, New York, NY 10104
Visit us at lb-kids.com

Little, Brown and Company is a division of Hachette Book Group, Inc.
The Little, Brown name and logo are trademarks of Hachette Book Group, Inc.

The publisher is not responsible for websites (or their content) that are not owned by the publisher.

First Paperback Edition: October 2016
First published in hardcover in October 2007 by Little, Brown and Company

Library of Congress Control Number: 2007300204

Hardcover ISBN 978-0-316-16686-7—Paperback ISBN 978-0-316-35224-6

10 9 8 7 6 5 4 3 2 1

APS

PRINTED IN CHINA

The illustrations for this book were done in watercolor.
The text was set in Optima, and the display type was set in Orange Grove.

To Brett

Christmas was just around the corner, and Puddle hadn't seen a single snowflake yet. Just let it snow, he wistfully pleaded to the sky. There had to be snow!

His friend Toot was more concerned about another matter altogether. He wanted to give Puddle a wonderful surprise for Christmas, the best present ever.

He knew that the best present was usually something you made yourself, a one-of-kind thingamajig, not just a whatsit anyone could buy in a store.

One year he made Puddle a bright red sled.
They named it the W. P. Rocket.

Another year he gave his pal a mysterious
seedpod. They waited half the winter to see
how it would bloom.

And just last Christmas he presented Puddle with a real raft, big enough for two: The W. P. Pond Lily Queen. They couldn't wait until spring to launch it.

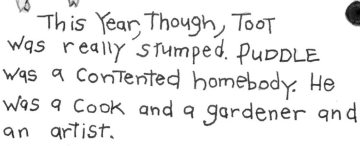

This year, though, Toot was really stumped. PUDDLE was a contented homebody. He was a cook and a gardener and an artist.

He loved trees and birds and his own backyard. He was certainly the best friend you could have. What could he possibly give good old Puds for

CHRISTMAS?

COOK

Gardener

Artist

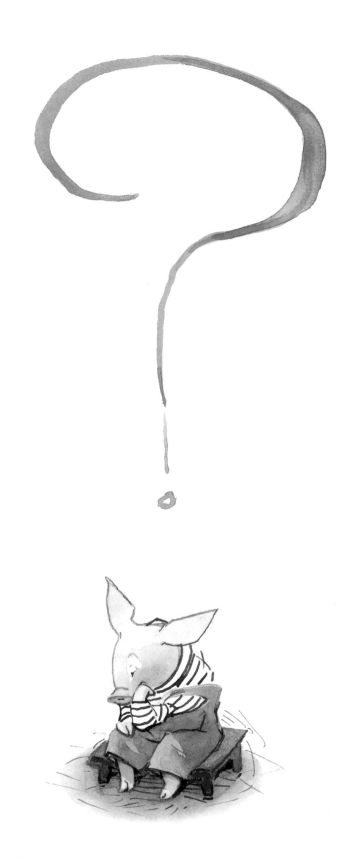

Of course, Puddle was asking himself the same question about Toot.

One year he knit him a wool sweater, robin-egg blue.

Another Christmas he gave him a purple ball for balancing on.

Then there was the year of Puddle's giant plum pudding, which kept them merrily stuffed for a month.

Puddle knew Toot inside out. His friend loved hiking and adventuring and strange places. He loved maps and gear and exciting weather. He was brave and daring and jolly. He was the best friend ever. What was just the thing for good old Tootles this year?

When Puddle phoned his cousin Opal to ask her opinion, she said, "A little cuddly something would be nice, like a homemade doll."

"For Toot? Really?" asked Puddle.

"I think he'd like that," Opal replied sweetly.

When Toot called Opal with the same question concerning Puddle,
she said the same thing. "Maybe a homemade doll of some kind."

"A doll?" Toot was puzzled.

"Something soft and cute," she said.

That night it began to snow.

The next morning Toot and Puddle awoke to a new world. The snow that had been silently falling through the night now blanketed everything with a hushed, gleaming luster.

"The skis," Toot called. "Where are the skis?"

"I've got them," Puddle cried eagerly. "Let's go!"

The path through the woods became a magical journey. The two friends skied along in silence, stirred by the beauty surrounding them.

When they stopped to rest, Puddle said, "I wish I could take this morning and put it in my pocket and keep it forever."

"Me, too," Toot sighed. "It's perfect."

But then by evening, hard rain began to fall—"Oh no!" Puddle protested—and by the next day, the glorious snow was gone.

"I can't believe it." Toot frowned.

"Neither can I," Puddle said sadly. "I was all set to go sledding." His spirits had been momentarily dampened.

Still, Christmas was coming. It was almost here—snow or no snow!—and the two friends soon plunged into a state of busy excitement.

As for presents, Toot spent every spare minute in his workshop, in the basement, clearly inspired at last.

And Puddle was up to something equally private and absorbing in the attic.

DO NOT DISTURB

On Christmas Eve, the two friends emerged from their workrooms,
and each of them carried a handsomely wrapped something or other.
"Wouldn't you like to open your present right now?" Toot asked.
"We have to wait until tomorrow," Puddle said, "when Opal comes."

Christmas morning in Woodcock Pocket was brimming with anticipation. Opal soon arrived. As the youngest, she was the first to open presents.

"How did you know what I wanted?" she wondered appreciatively.

"It was just a lucky guess," said Puddle. "What will you name them?"

"Well," said Opal, "I'll have to get to know them first. One is probably a Toot and one is probably a Puddle."

"What is *a Puddle*?" Puddle asked.

"And what in the world is *a Toot*?" said Toot.

"You know," Opal replied. "I'm sure they're best friends, but one is one way and one is the other."

"Oh," said the friends together.

"Merry Christmas," Toot beamed, presenting his enormous gift to Puddle.
His friend unwrapped the package slowly and carefully.
"I love it," said Puddle.
"I made it myself," Toot said proudly.
"I know."
"It's for sledding—snow or no snow."
"Let's go sledding today," said Opal.

"And Merry Christmas to you," Puddle said, presenting his package.
Toot tried to remain calm, but couldn't quite suppress his eagerness.

"It's you and me," said Puddle shyly. He added, "That snowy day in the woods."

"It's perfect," Toot said, standing back to admire his friend's work. "There we are."